MW00875947

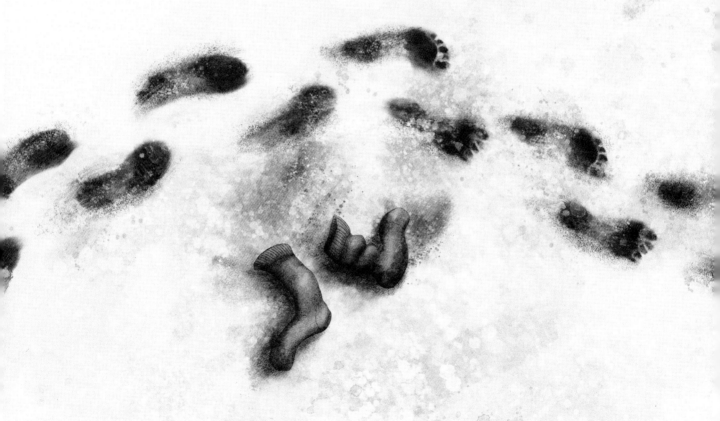

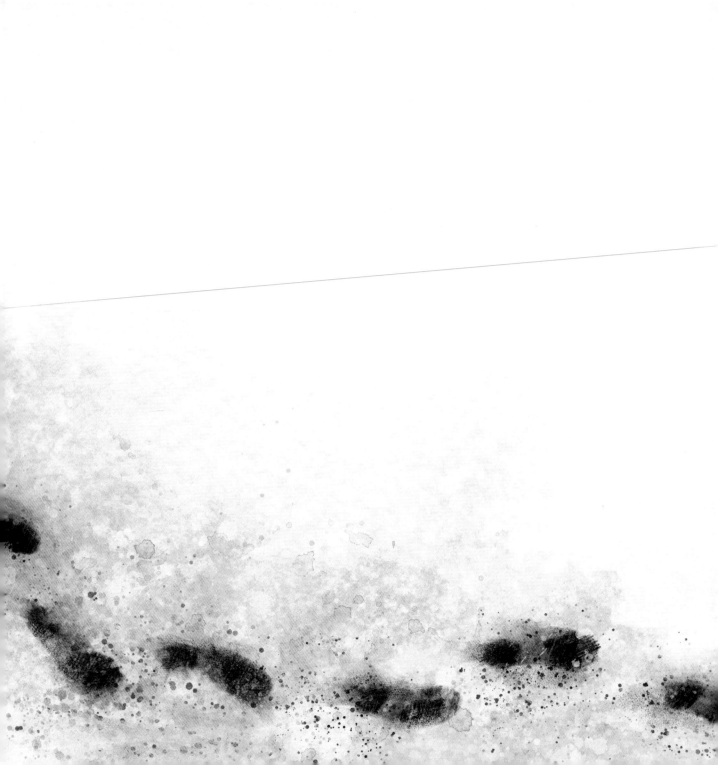

Quiet as Mud

by Jane Yolen

illustrated by Nicole Wong

Magination Press • Washington, DC
American Psychological Association

For Kristine and her son—*JY*

For I.A.U.—*NW*

Quiet As Mud is inspired by a quote from Margaret Wise Brown
in *The Radical Woman Behind "Goodnight Moon"*, an article in
The New Yorker by Anna Holmes, published January 31, 2022.

Magination Press
Books for Kids From the
American Psychological Association

Magination Press is a registered trademark of the American Psychological Association.
Order books at maginationpress.org, or call 1-800-374-2721.

Book design by Christina Gaugler
Printed by Phoenix Color, Hagerstown, MD

Library of Congress Cataloging-in-Publication Data
Names: Yolen, Jane, author. | Wong, Nicole (Nicole E.), illustrator.
Title: Quiet as mud / by Jane Yolen; illustrated by Nicole Wong.
Description: Washington, DC : Magination Press, [2024] | "American Psychological Association." | Summary: "Quiet as Mud is a sweet poem about being introvert in a big loud world"— Provided by publisher.
Identifiers: LCCN 2023019320 (print) | LCCN 2023019321 (ebook) | ISBN 9781433841538 (hardcover) | ISBN 9781433841545 (ebook)
Subjects: LCSH: Children's poetry, American. | Quietude—Juvenile poetry. | CYAC: Quietude—Poetry. | American poetry. | LCGFT: Poetry. | Picture books.
Classification: LCC PS3575.O43 Q54 2024 (print) | LCC PS3575.O43 (ebook) | DDC 811/.54—dc23/eng/20230613
LC record available at https://lccn.loc.gov/2023019320 | LC ebook record available at https://lccn.loc.gov/2023019321

Manufactured in the United States of America
10 9 8 7 6 5 4 3 2 1

"Here, perhaps, is the stage of rhyme and reason...

'Big as the whole world,'
'Deep as a giant,'
'Quiet as electricity rushing about the world,'
'Quiet as mud.'

All these are five-year-old similes.
Let the grown-up writer for children
equal or better them if he can."

—Margaret Wise Brown

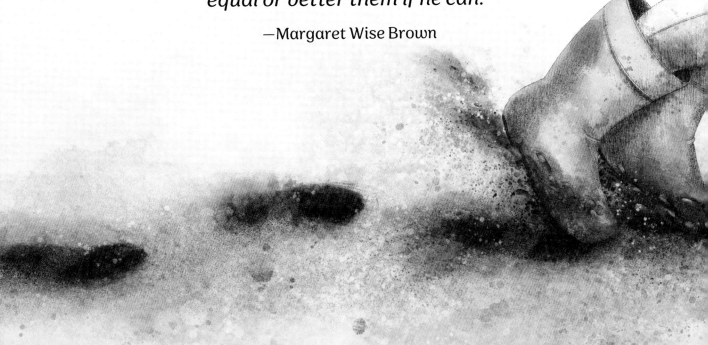

My little sister says I'm quiet as the stars.

Mama says I'm silent as a stone.

My big brother says I whisper like the forest.

But I'm quiet as mud when I'm alone.

My daddy says that I am silent as a sandwich
when it sits uneaten on a plate.

Granny says I sound as hushed as a snail,
as it slimes its way across a crate.

My Uncle George says I talk less than the moon
as it keeps its watch above the sea.

My Aunt Alice says I'm caught in a dream.
But it all seems real enough to me.

I just like hearing the world spin by.

And the songs that the rocks all sing.
I like to think of words that could go along,

and the heavy way the winds all ring.

It makes me happy to hear my heart beat,
with its own steady thud-thud-thud.

As I sit in the rocker and listen to the world,
and I stay as quiet as mud.

Jane Yolen is the author of over 400 books for children and adults. Her books, stories, and poems have won many awards including the Caldecott Medal, two Nebula Awards, two Christopher Medals, three Golden Kite Awards, and the Jewish Book Award. She lives in Hatfield, MA. Visit janeyolen.com, @Jane.Yolen on Facebook, @JaneYolen on Twitter, and @JYolen on Instagram.

Nicole Wong is a graduate of the Rhode Island School of Design. Nicole lives in Massachusetts. Visit nicole-wong.com, and @PainterNik9 on Instagram.

Magination Press is the children's book imprint of the American Psychological Association. It's the combined power of psychology and literature that makes a Magination Press book special. Visit maginationpress.org and @MaginationPress on Facebook, Twitter, Instagram, and Pinterest.